BARYSHNIKOV'S
Nutcracker

BARYSHNIKOV'S NUTCRACKER

by
NORMA KLEIN

With Photographs by
KEN REGAN

Additional Photographs by
CHRISTOPHER LITTLE and MARTHA SWOPE

Choreography by
MIKHAIL BARYSHNIKOV

Music by
PETER ILYICH TCHAIKOVSKY

Starring
MIKHAIL BARYSHNIKOV and GELSEY KIRKLAND
with ALEXANDER MINZ

Produced and Written for Television by
YANNA KROYT BRANDT

Directed by
TONY CHARMOLI

Production Designed by
BORIS ARONSON

Executive Producer
HERMAN KRAWITZ

Based on the AMERICAN BALLET THEATRE Television Production
Lucia Chase and Oliver Smith, co-Directors

G. P. PUTNAM'S SONS New York

Library of Congress Cataloging in Publication Data

Klein, Norma, date.
  Baryshnikov's Nutcracker.

  "Based on the American Ballet Theatre production.
Choreography by Mikhail Baryshnikov."
  1. The nutcracker (Ballet) I. Baryshnikov, Mikhail,
date. II. Regan, Ken. III. Little, Christopher.
IV. Tchaikovsky, Peter Ilich, 1840–1893. Shchelkunchik.
V. American Ballet Theatre. VI. Title.
GV1790.N8K58 1983   792.8'42   83-11174
ISBN 0-399-12887-5

BOOK DESIGN BY BERNARD SCHLEIFER

Printed in the United States of America

"LET ME SEE!" I tried pushing Fritz out of the way, but he shoved me aside. He's fourteen, two years older than I am, and stronger. When we were little, we used to play together a lot, but in the last year or so I don't like to as much. He treats me like a baby, acting as though everything he was interested in was so much better than the things I care about.

Every Christmas Eve our parents give a big party. They decorate the tree, and at the last minute, when everything is done, we are allowed to come in. Of course, I know what it will look like—Mama uses the same decorations every year. But since I only see them once a year, they seem special. Some of my friends get to trim the tree themselves, but in a way I like it this way, having it just appear, fully decorated, as a surprise. The ornaments are beautiful—little glass animals, colored balls, china dolls, and real candles, which Papa watches carefully to make sure they don't start a fire. One Christmas a scary thing happened. I leaned too close to one of the candles, and my hair caught fire! I screamed, but by the time Mama got there, it had gone out. There was just a little charred end, which she trimmed off. But ever since then I'm very careful when I come close to the tree.

Fritz stepped away for a moment, and I quickly peeked through the keyhole. You can't really see much, and I know they won't let us in, but it's fun to try. I think I saw Mama's bright orange dress, but it was hard to tell.

"I'm going upstairs to change," I told Fritz. "Tell Mama if she comes out."

"Change to what?" he said.

"Another dress."

"You're crazy."

He's right. I guess I am a little crazy about this. But I want to look just right. Not only pretty but grown-up. What I wish more than anything is that Mama would let me join in the dancing. I can dance so well! I've taken lessons for years. She says I have to wait until I'm really grown-up, till I'm sixteen. She still thinks of me as a little girl, the way I used to be. I have to wear my hair loose, not swept up in a fancy style the way she does. Oh, I know the time will come, but I feel so impatient. I can't wait four more years. This year my cousin Sophie will be sixteen and she will get to dance for the first time. She promises to tell me what it is like.

On Christmas itself we visit Sophie's parents, my Aunt and Uncle, and exchange presents, then we have a huge Christmas dinner. I like Sophie. Even though she's four years older than I, she's so much friendlier than Fritz.

I went to my room. It's pretty. I have a big doll house and a special cupboard for all my dolls. Some of them are so fancy I'm not supposed to play with them. They're like statues. They just sit there, looking a little haughty, as though they wonder what they're doing in a little girl's room. But then there are a few that I've played with so much they're all worn out. I used to sleep with one, Claire, and her hair rubbed off in the back, like an old man going bald, but I still love her. I bet this year they'll give me another doll. It's not that I don't want one, but I wish they'd give me a present that showed they thought of me as more grown-up. I won't throw my dolls out, the way my friend Sara did, but they don't mean as much to me as they used to. They seem babyish. Mama says that's a sign I'm ready to think of having babies of my own, instead of pretend ones. No, I'm not ready for that! I think I'm somewhere in between.

I couldn't decide among my three best dresses. One is white with peach trim in the front. That's the newest. It has a long full skirt and it's really pretty. The second is pale blue. I think blue is my best color—it matches my eyes—but I wore that dress last year. The third, which I'm wearing, is one Sophie gave me when it got too small for her. It's all white, covered with lace. The trouble is, I always think of it as Sophie's dress because I know she wore it first. Not that it's shabby, but it wasn't one made especially for me. Mama says it's silly to think of it like that. She was the youngest of all her sisters and wore dozens of hand-me-downs.

I walked to the mirror and held the other dresses in turn against me. Maybe the white one with the peach trim is the best. Mama would be hurt if I didn't wear it. She had it made just for me. I had to go for four fittings. I took off Sophie's dress and put on the new one, being especially careful as it went over my head.

"Clara, what are you doing?" It was Mama, standing in the doorway of my room, looking cross.

"I'm changing my dress," I said, looking at her with a melting expression. "Will you do up my buttons?"

"Of course. But I thought you'd decided on Sophie's dress." As I came close to Mama, I could smell the perfume that she always wears on special occasions. I like it when she helps me get dressed. Her hands are so soft and light. When she was finished, she said, "Now let's find a ribbon to match."

Together we picked a ribbon, and she tied it carefully around my hair. I have long blond hair, not quite to my waist, but almost. I love the way it feels when I wear it loose like this. I cried when Mama made me cut it a few inches, so it would be easier to brush. "How do I look?" I asked when she was done.

"Lovely. . . . You'll be the prettiest little girl at the party."

I turned away. I'd wanted her to say "the prettiest young lady." "Mama, can't I put my hair up? I look so young this way." I pulled it back and showed her how it would look that way.

"I've told you, darling, you're not old enough. You'd just look silly. And your hair is so pretty loose."

"I don't see why I can't stay up and dance," I said mournfully. "I'm just as good a dancer as Sophie is!"

"Of course you are," Mama said soothingly. "And it will make it all the more exciting when you do it for the first time."

When Mama went to her first dance at sixteen, she met my father, and right in the middle of dancing a waltz together, they fell in love! Isn't that romantic? I want it to happen like that for me, but Mama says I shouldn't worry if it doesn't. Sometimes it takes longer. Sometimes women are fussy like my Aunt Helen and turn down many men who want to marry them.

"Here I thought you'd be so excited to see the tree," Mama said, "and you're just moping around in your room."

"It is ready?" I asked excitedly. I'd forgotten all about the tree.

"It is . . . Come." She took my hand, and we went downstairs together.

The afternoon of Christmas Eve, Papa drives with our coachman to the forest, and they pick the biggest, tallest fir tree they can find—so big that the woodcutter has to chop it down and bring it to our house in a special carriage. Luckily, the ceiling in our living room is very high. There has to be room at the top for the angel.

I ran into the living room so fast my slippers skidded on the floor. The floors were polished as they always are when there's going to be dancing. "It's beautiful," I said to Papa. "It's the nicest one of all." It's funny—each year Papa gets a different kind of fir tree, and each year I think that one is the nicest. I like the kind with thick, furry branches. The ornaments seem to be peeking out from deep in the tree. I imagine that some of them are shy, the way I used to be. They're glad to be there, but they don't all want to hang out on the tips of branches. Some are pleased to snuggle deep back where they can watch everything that's happening. When I was little, I used to have names for all the ornaments. I would sit on the floor with Fritz, and we would make up adventures for them all. We wouldn't take them off the tree, but we would describe what they were doing and where they had been since the previous Christmas. That was before Fritz got so interested in soldiers. That's all he's interested in now, setting them up for fights. He says he hopes there's a war so he can go off and be a real soldier some day. Isn't that stupid? What if he were killed? But he doesn't think of that, just how handsome he'll look in his uniform and how brave he'll be rescuing people.

Guests started arriving, a lot of our relatives, and many of Mama and Papa's friends. I stood to the side, watching, when suddenly I felt a hand over my eyes. Normally I would have been scared, but I knew who it must be. "Uncle D.!" I cried and put my hand over his.

It *was* him. I love my Uncle Drosselmeyer best of all my relatives. He's my mother's only brother and he's never been married, though he likes pretty women and often brings them to dinner. He loves children and says he pretends that I'm his daughter because I'm just the way he would like his own little girl to be if he had one. I'm not boasting—he really says that. "What are you wearing?" I said. He had on a tall black hat covered with silver stars and a black suit with a big black cape.

"My Christmas costume," he said, smiling. "Do I look handsome?"

"You look scary," I said, "like a magician."

"Not scary," he said. "Mysterious. . . . And you—look what a young lady you've become! Next thing you'll have your hair up and will be dancing all over the place."

"They won't let me, not for four more years," I said.

"Well, you save me the first dance," he said. "Remember?"

"I'll remember."

"I have a special present for you," he went on.

"Give it to me now!" I cried. Uncle D.'s presents are wonderful, much more exciting and interesting than the kind most people give. He would never give me a doll, for instance.

He held up his hand. "Not so impatient, little Clara," he said. "First I have a few other treats for all the children."

Little Clara! Just after he'd said I looked like a young lady! I moved back against the tree and watched the grown-ups. Mama was dancing with Papa. He looked handsome with his dark moustache and beard, and Mama was so pretty in her orange dress. She likes bright colors and says she wants to wear them always, even when she's an old lady. Underneath her dress is the most wonderful petticoat made of horsehair covered with lace. It makes her dress stand out and gives her such a tiny waist. Papa isn't a good dancer. He bounces up and down with a lot of energy, but he doesn't glide smoothly and gracefully the way you're supposed to. But Mama looks as though she doesn't care. She could have married a better dancer, but she fell in love with Papa anyway, even though she said the first time he kissed her, his beard tickled her chin and made her laugh. He thought she didn't like his kisses!

"Now time for the puppet show," Uncle D. called out when the music had stopped for a moment.

We all gathered around, all my cousins, even Fritz and his friends. Uncle's marionettes are famous, they look so real and move so nimbly. The story was about a Prince and a Mouse King, who were having a fight. The mouse was big, as big as the Prince, and very fierce looking. In my head I made up a story about them. I knew the Prince would win, but I still felt scared as I watched.

Sophie was sitting next to me. Even though she's sixteen, she still likes puppet shows. "Ugh, how real that mouse is," she said.

"I hope he wins," Fritz said. "Get him, Mousie!"

I kicked him. "Hush."

The Princess marionette stood to one side, her eyes big and frightened looking. At the end she and the Prince got into a golden sleigh and rode off together. Then Uncle came out from behind the stage.

"Where did you get such a terrible looking puppet?" Sophie said, picking up the Mouse King.

"I made it," Uncle D. said. "He's my favorite. I worked a long time on him. Did he really scare you?"

"Yes!" She looked at me and I nodded.

"There should be a Mouse Queen, too," I said.

"There should be," he agreed. "You're right. Next year I'll make a Mouse Queen and that will explain how the Mouse King and the Prince came to hate each other so much."

While we were looking at the marionettes, Fritz and his friends started a mock fight, pretending to be soldiers. They had pretend swords and they dodged back and forth with them, falling to the ground if they were hit. Uncle D. went over and grabbed Fritz round the waist. "Don't you want to see the rest of the show?" he asked.

Whenever Uncle talks, even Fritz becomes quiet. He and his friends sat down quietly while Uncle got the next part of the show ready. He brought out two big dolls, a harlequin and a female harlequin. First the harlequin danced. He did somersaults so fast you could hardly see him! Then the lady harlequin came out and danced alone, and then they danced together. She had big pink spots on her cheeks, but she was pretty anyway. When she was finished, she slumped over, and Uncle carried her off to a corner. Quietly I went over and touched her dress.

"Don't you want to see the Moor?" Uncle asked.

"Oh yes." I hurried back to my place beside Sophie.

The Moor was strange looking. He had a turban and bright orange gloves and very fierce looking dark eyes. He danced in a funny way, leaping high in the air, his legs spread way far out. Papa has a book with illustrations of Moorish people who look like that. He said the men always wear that kind of hat, though I suppose they take it off when they go to sleep.

"Now the presents," Sophie whispered to me.

All the children gathered around in a circle, and Papa reached into a big sack and called out our names. Sometimes someone's name would come up twice in a row, and he would say, "Another present for Clara? How can that be?" I got so many nice things—one was a special painted fan from Mama that comes from China. When you open it up wide, you can see a scene of women crossing a bridge.

"It's to flirt with," Sophie said. She showed me how, holding it up so you could just see her eyes.

"Do you have one?" I asked.

"Three . . . And I'm just learning how to use them. They really work! They make you look very mysterious."

I did get a doll, just as I'd expected, from one of my aunts. It had bright pink cheeks and round eyes. "I'm beginning to hate dolls," I confessed to Sophie.

"Oh, but she's such a pretty one. Look, her eyes open and shut."

I was surprised that Sophie, at her age, could still like dolls. She says she collects them, not to play with, but to decorate her room. Mama and Papa gave me a string of pearls and some earrings. Sophie got a bottle of perfume and she dabbed some behind my ears.

"Do you have boyfriends yet?" I asked her.

"No one special. . . . Look at that man over there. Isn't he handsome? Who is he?"

I didn't know. "Maybe he'll ask you to dance," I said.

"I hope so . . . I have to do my magic trick. Watch!"

I watched while Sophie lifted up the fan and started staring hard at the man who was halfway across the room. He looked at us once and then away, but a moment or two later he looked back again. It's funny that you can flirt with someone from across the room. That must take practice. Pretty soon he came over and asked Sophie to dance, just as she'd wanted. She gave me a smile as she stood up, and off they went!

"How did you like your presents?" Uncle D. asked.

"Very much." Then I remembered. "But you said you had a special gift for me. Where is it?"

"I thought you'd forgotten all about it, Clara dear. Come with me."

I followed him into a corner of the room so we wouldn't get in the way of the dancers.

"Close your eyes," he said.

I did, and waited patiently till he touched my shoulder lightly. "Now you can look."

I opened my eyes. At first I was disappointed. There, standing in the middle of the floor, was a wooden doll about a foot high. He looked like some of Fritz's soldiers. In fact, he was a little ugly, with a big square jaw and a fierce expression. "What is it?" I asked, trying not to show how I felt.

"This is Nutcracker . . . Nutcracker, Clara, my favorite niece. She is here to take care of you." To me he said with a smile, "Come closer. He doesn't bite. All he does is crack nuts."

I went over and touched the Nutcracker. It was true—as I came closer, I saw that he had a friendly expression in his green eyes, almost as though he wanted to smile but couldn't. I liked him, liked him very much, in fact. "Does he really crack nuts?" I asked.

"Certainly." Uncle D. reached into his pocket and drew out a handful. He put one in the Nutcracker's mouth. "Now, young man," he said, "show us what you can do." The Nutcracker's mouth came down and out popped the nut, neatly split down the center.

I took the nut and ate it. "Thank you," I told him. I looked at my Uncle. "But can I play with him? Or is he just to use for cracking nuts?"

"Of course you can play with him," Uncle D. said. "He is yours."

I reached out and held the Nutcracker in my arms. "He has a funny face," I said. "I suppose he has to have such a big jaw so he can crack the nuts."

"Yes," Unce D. said, "I'm afraid the poor fellow will have a hard time finding a girlfriend with a face like that."

"Maybe there's a female nutcracker," I suggested.

"No, no such thing," Uncle said. "He'll just have to go through life alone."

"Like you?" I suggested.

"Me? Never! You think I'm as funny looking as my puppets, do you? Never fear. One day I'll come home with the most beautiful bride of all."

I hope, for Uncle's sake, that he does, but I know I'll feel jealous in a way . . . especially if he has children and pays more attention to them than he does to me. I looked back at the Nutcracker who was looking at us with such an intelligent expression, as though he understood everything we were saying. "I'll be his girlfriend," I said. "I think he's handsome."

"You see," Uncle said. "He looks more handsome already. That's what every man is waiting for—a lovely young girl who will like his looks, no matter what they happen to be."

"When I first saw him," I admitted, "I thought he was a soldier, like the ones Fritz plays with."

"No," Uncle said. "This Nutcracker is a kind, gentle soul. He doesn't like fighting." He stuck out his hand and pretended to shake the Nutcracker's hand. "I have to ask you, kind sir, if you'll permit me to have the hand of this beautiful lady for the next dance."

"He says yes," I said eagerly, setting Nutcracker down on the floor.

Every Christmas Eve Uncle lets me have one dance with him, at the very end of the evening. He always apologizes about his dancing. "I should take lessons," he says. "I'm so clumsy compared to you, Clara. Dancing with you is like dancing with a feather."

We danced around and around the room. I saw Mama's orange dress whirl by. Then I caught sight of Sophie, who was still dancing with the young man she'd been peeking at behind the fan. "Has it been a nice Christmas Eve party for you?" Uncle asked. "Did you like your presents?"

I nodded. "They were all beautiful."

"Which was your favorite?"

I hesitated. "Oh, of course I liked the necklace and earrings Papa and Mama gave me, and the fan . . . but best of all I think I liked the Nutcracker."

Uncle smiled. "I thought you were getting too old for dolls."

"He's not a doll, really," I said. It was hard to explain. "He looks like a real person, if you look into his eyes."

Everyone says that is the secret of Uncle's puppets, that he makes their expressions so real. Mama says he is a true artist, but, of course, he couldn't earn a living making puppets so he just does it as a hobby. He told me once that while he is working on them, they begin to seem real to him, too. Sometimes, he said, he even talks to them as he works.

Uncle bowed. "Thank you, my dear," he said. "You get lighter and more graceful every year. . . . Hey, what's this?"

We both went over to the corner of the room where Fritz and his friends were playing with my Nutcracker. They were feeding nuts into his mouth and popping them out one after another. Snap, snap, like bullets.

"Stop!" I cried. "You'll break him. . . . Uncle, make them stop. It's my present."

"Yours?" said one of the friends, a tall, fierce looking young man. "He's a soldier! What do you want with him?"

"He's not. He hates fighting." I tried to get the Nutcracker away from the guest, but he was too quick for me. The Nutcracker smashed on the floor and his head came off. I started to cry.

I held up the Nutcracker to Uncle. "He's broken. Look, his head came off." I could hardly speak, I was crying so much.

Uncle D. glared at Fritz. "You are a spoiled, foolish boy," he said. "How dare you touch Clara's present without asking?"

Fritz looked sulky and angry. "I didn't do it. It was him," he said, pointing at a guest who was moving away through the crowd.

"This is a toy that took me many hours to make," Uncle D. said. He took the Nutcracker, his head and body, from me. With one gesture he fitted the head back onto the body. "Fortunately he is well made so no harm is done. There, Clara. Your little man is fine again."

I took the Nutcracker and turned him over carefully. He really seemed to be as good as new, but his face looked sad to me, as though he still hurt from being handled so roughly.

"Here," Uncle said, handing me his handkerchief. "You tie that around his neck. It will make him feel better."

I took the handkerchief and tied it carefully. "Thank you," I said. I still felt bad to have the Nutcracker start his life in our house in such a terrible way. "If you go near him again," I said to Fritz, "I'll take all your soldiers and bury them in a hole in the middle of the forest and you'll never see them again!"

"I don't want him," Fritz said. "Take it easy. He's just an old ugly nutcracker. He can't even crack nuts well."

The party was ending. Mama and Papa stood against the wall, shaking hands with all their guests and listening to everyone say what a wonderful party it had been. Sophie glided by me. She was wearing her velvet coat trimmed with fur. She looked like a princess. "I'll tell you everything tomorrow," she said, kissing me. "Sleep well."

I was getting sleepy, but I waited up until the last guest had left. Mama seemed surprised to see me. "I thought you went in hours ago," she said. "Quick, be off with you."

Usually we leave all our presents under the tree on Christmas Eve night, but I hated leaving the Nutcracker after he'd had such a scare. I went to my room and changed into my nightgown, then went downstairs again. Papa was dousing the candles one by one. The ornaments seemed to disappear as he put out one light after the other. I took the Nutcracker and set him carefully in one of my doll beds. I covered him with a blanket. "Sleep well," I told him. "I'll see you in the morning. Tomorrow is Christmas, and we'll go to Sophie's house. You haven't met her yet, but she's very nice . . ."

I would have stayed and talked to him longer, but Papa said, "Time for bed" and scooped me up and carried me upstairs. It used to be easy for him to carry me. Now that I'm big he has to go slowly, and when he finally placed me on my bed, he looked out of breath. "This is the last Christmas I can do that, I'm afraid," he said.

I got under the covers. "Why is Fritz so noisy?" I asked.

"Well, it's his age," Papa said. "He'll get over it. When you're both grown up, you'll be the best of friends. You won't even remember that you fought at all."

I know that isn't true! I know I'll remember forever.

"When you get older, he'll introduce you to his friends. They can take you to dances. You'll be glad to have an older brother." He bent down to kiss me. "Merry Christmas," he said softly.

After Papa left, I lay quietly in bed, looking around my room. All the dolls were asleep on their shelf. I thought of the Nutcracker downstairs in the big living room. How lonely he must feel, all by himself in a strange house, not knowing anyone. In the morning I would introduce him to all the other dolls. That way he'd have someone to talk to when I wasn't with him.

Then I had an idea. I decided to sneak downstairs and see how he was doing. It was hard getting out of bed. I felt so warm and snug I didn't want to move. I tiptoed as quietly as I could out of my room and down the big, big staircase. Mama and Papa's room is far down the hall, and they always close their door. I knew they wouldn't hear me. But it was scary. The stairs were dark except for the two lights that burn all night long. The floor felt cold.

Slowly I opened the door to the living room. The tree looked enormous, even bigger than it had earlier. I could hardly see the gold angel at the top, and all the decorations were just little dark shapes, hardly distinguishable. I crept over to the tree and found the Nutcracker wrapped in his blanket. He looked calm, not frightened the way he had before, but his big eyes were open, as though he'd had trouble falling asleep and was hoping I would come down.

"Are you comfortable?" I asked in a whisper. "How does your neck feel?" I touched his neck, and he looked at me as though to say it didn't hurt anymore. I tried to explain to him.

". . . Anyway, Fritz won't bother you again. After tomorrow you can sleep upstairs in my room. There'll be lots of toys and dolls for you to talk to when I'm not there. I don't want you to be lonely."

I looked down at the Nutcracker's face. His eyes were fastened right on mine. He understood everything I was saying, I could tell. "I was hoping I would get something special for Christmas," I said. "I'm getting tired of my dolls. They're nice, but they're boring after a while. Some of them are really beautiful, though."

I wonder how the Nutcracker feels about the way he looks. I wonder if he ever catches sight of himself in the mirror and wishes he had a different face. I always do that! Sometimes I wish I looked like Mama or Sophie, that I had milk-white skin and a beautiful figure. Of course, the Nutcracker's jaw has to be big and strong so he can crack nuts, and that's what gives him a funny expression. I opened his jaw and put my finger in, but he didn't bite me. You can tell he would never bite or fight unless someone attacked him.

"I can introduce you to some of the decorations on the tree," I whispered. "Would you like that? They have names, all of them, and I once wrote them all down." I looked up at the tree and saw a few way back deep in the branches. "Do you see those two?" I said. "The doll with the white hair and the boy with the cane? Those are Sylvia and Stefan. They take care of a flock of sheep during the day. That's why Stefan has that cane. It's to poke the sheep with, when they won't move . . ."

Several of the decorations I wanted the Nutcracker to meet were up so high, I wasn't sure he could see them, and I looked for a few that were closer. One was a little gray mouse in a red coat. I call him Sylvester. Carefully I unhooked him from the branch and brought him over to the Nutcracker's bed. "This is Sylvester," I said. "He was once caught in a trap that Papa put out because Papa hates mice, but Sylvester managed to get free." I looked at the Nutcracker's face, and he looked frightened.

"He's not a bad mouse," I assured him. "You don't have to worry." But he still looked as though he wished I would take him away, so I did. I know how the Nutcracker feels. I don't like mice either, not real ones. But Sylvester is so small and soft and friendly looking. If you press his stomach, he lets out a little squeak.

Then I found the prettiest doll of all. She has wings, but she's not an angel. Her dress is so light and pink, it looks like it's made of sugar. "Isn't she beautiful?" I said. "I used to think she could grant wishes, but now I'm not sure. One year I asked for a special wish, and it came true! But the next year it didn't. Maybe she only makes wishes come true that she thinks are good ones. You could try if you want."

I wondered what the Nutcracker would wish. Would he wish to be a real person so he could talk and move and dance and do everything people can do? I was getting so sleepy, sitting here, but I didn't feel cold or afraid anymore. I was glad I'd come down to keep the Nutcracker company. Then suddenly the big grandfather clock began to chime midnight. At the top of the clock is a golden owl whose wings droop down over the top. The strangest thing happened. Suddenly the owl's face turned into my Uncle's! I was so startled to see him up there that I jumped. His eyes looked so dark and intense. "Uncle, what are you doing up there?" I called out.

But he didn't answer. His mouth was open, and each time the clock chimed, he said, "Clara! Clara!" as though he was calling me. I grabbed the Nutcracker up in my arms, and we sat huddled together, frightened. Then the clock finished all its chimes, and my Uncle's face faded away. It was just the owl again.

"Did you see that?" I asked the Nutcracker. "Why was he there? He should be home asleep."

The Nutcracker looked at me with such a sympathetic expression, as though he couldn't understand either. "Now you'll think we have a very strange house," I said, "with all kinds of odd things happening all the time. But it's not so. Papa and Mama are very nice, regular people." I yawned. "I'm getting so sleepy, Nutcracker. Do you need me to stay with you longer? We can sleep together here, under the tree. Would you like that?"

I could tell that that was exactly what the Nutcracker wanted. As soon as I curled up on the floor, holding him in my arms, he gave a smile and even closed his eyes, as though finally he felt safe. "Sleep well," I whispered. "I'll be here with you all night."

I DON'T KNOW HOW LONG I slept, but when I woke up, the Nutcracker was no longer in my arms. I thought perhaps he'd been uncomfortable, but when I looked in his bed, he wasn't there either.

"Nutcracker?" I called. "Where are you?" It was still dark, and I was afraid to speak too loudly in the big room for fear Mama and Papa would hear me and make me go back to bed. Suddenly I wondered if Fritz had gotten up and stolen the Nutcracker just to tease me.

But just then I heard a soft scuffling noise coming from behind the tree. "Who is it?" I called, my heart beating so rapidly it was hard to speak.

There was no answer. But a moment later a large gray mouse came dancing out and stood, almost like a statue, in front of the tree. I don't think he even saw me, but I shrank back out of his sight. He had soft, velvety looking gray fur and big, sparkling dark eyes. I wondered why I didn't feel more scared since usually I hate mice. Instead I just watched him in wonder as he pranced nimbly all around the big room, as though he was pleased to be there. I suppose mice are cooped up all the time, always hiding in corners, trying to avoid being caught in traps. Maybe it's only at night that they feel brave enough to come out. If I hadn't come downstairs to see the Nutcracker, I'd never have seen him.

But then, a moment later, another mouse came out, and then another. Goodness, how many were there? I tried to count, but they were moving around so rapidly it was hard. Eight, nine, ten. And all as big as the first one! Were they hungry? Was that why they had come out? Perhaps they were disappointed that, on Christmas Eve, no one had thought to leave them any presents. I wondered if I should rush to the kitchen and see if there were any extra pieces of cheese they might like. But they were so big! Surely Mama didn't have that much cheese.

The mice were running all around the room, boldly, as though it was their house and I was the intruder. I began to wish I was back in bed. Perhaps while they weren't looking, I could sneak up the stairs. Moving very quietly, I tiptoed around the back of the tree and started towards the stairs, when suddenly I ran straight into someone. It was the Nutcracker! But he was as big as I, bigger even, and had a sword dangling at his side. Without even thinking I jumped into his arms, and he caught me and held me close to him.

He wasn't made of wood anymore; he felt like a real person, though his face was still the same: stern, but friendly. "Oh, Nutcracker, I was so frightened! I didn't know where you'd gone," I said, clinging to him. "And suddenly all these mice appeared. Who are they? Why are they here?"

"They are our enemies," Nutcracker said. "They have come to fight."

I peered out at the mice, who were making loud squeaking noises. They sounded angry. "How *can* we fight them?" I said. "I don't know how to fight."

"Find Fritz's soldiers," he said. "They will help us."

"But will you be all right?" I asked. Just one Nutcracker against so many mice didn't seem fair.

"I can protect myself," he said. "I have my sword. . . . But *you* must be careful, Clara."

"But *I'm* not their enemy," I said. "I don't even know them."

He looked into my eyes. "But they know you are my dear friend, and they hate me. Therefore they will attack you, too."

I was happy that the Nutcracker called me his "dear friend." "But why do they hate you?" I asked.

He set me down gently. "Later," he said. "I will tell you everything later. Now go quickly. We have no time to lose."

I rushed up the stairs to Fritz's room, hoping the poor Nutcracker would manage with all those mice. Fritz was deeply, deeply asleep. I didn't worry about waking him. Mama says you can shoot a cannon near his ear and he won't wake up. I went to the cupboard where he keeps his soldiers and opened it up. "Come!" I whispered. "We need you downstairs. There's a terrible fight."

For a moment they all just lay there, tumbled about, they way they are when Fritz tosses them into the box. But then one by one they got up and, without even looking at me, marched out of the box and down the stairs. The minute they were out of the box, they grew and grew until, marching down the stairs, they were no longer toy soldiers, but real ones. Thank heavens! I had wondered how Fritz's tiny toy soldiers would be any help in fighting those giant mice. I thought of how angry Fritz would be in the morning that I had let him miss the first real fight of his life. But you could see he had his soldiers well trained. All those hours of making them march in formation had been well spent.

When we got downstairs, I saw the leader of the mice, the Mouse King. He was even bigger than the others. He looked just like the guest at the party who had played so roughly with the Nutcracker, but he wore a gold crown on his head, and a red cape flew from his shoulders. And my Nutcracker chased him from one end of the living room to another, his sword out, blazing. Seeing me with the soldiers, Nutcracker called out, "Bravo, Clara! Well done!" But the Mouse King glared at me, as though to say, "What is *she* doing here? Why can't she mind her own business?"

I had no sword, yet I hated to just stay by the sidelines watching the mice do battle with the soldiers. I crept out and pulled as hard as I could on the tail of one of the mice. He turned and, as he did, a soldier advanced on him and ran him through. Several other mice rushed out and pulled the body out of sight.

I thought how upset Mama would be in the morning, seeing all those giant mice lying around her living room. It amazed me that she could be sleeping through all this din when sometimes, if I play too loudly, she'll hear me from so far away. I sat back against the tree, and then I noticed that the decorations had crept out to the tips of the branches to watch. Stefan and Sylvia stood right near my arm, staring with horror as the fight continued.

"I wish I could help them," Stefan said.

"No, don't," Sylvia said, touching his arm. "You're not a soldier, just a shepherd. You could get hurt."

Stefan looked indignant. "What if the mice win?" he said. "They'll burn the tree to the ground. They'll eat all of us!"

"No," she cried. "You won't let them, will you, Clara?"

"Of course not," I said, but privately I wondered how I could stop them if the mice really were hungry. On the tree were little gingerbread men, candy canes, dolls made out of spun sugar. I imagined with horror the mice gobbling down all the beautiful decorations, setting the whole tree on fire.

"I think they are losing," Stefan said. "There don't seem to be as many of them."

"Perhaps they'll go and get more," Sylvia said. "Ugh, how ugly they are!"

I watched as my Nutcracker fought off several mice with his sword. Then he vanished behind a large sofa. Had he fallen? "I'll be back in a minute," I whispered to the two dolls and ran to where the Nutcracker had disappeared.

"Can you make it?" I asked. "Give me your sword! *I'll* fight!"

"No, this must be decided between me and the King. He has been my enemy for many, many years. If I don't vanquish him, I'm lost!" Saying that, the Nutcracker leaped to his feet and sprung out into the center of the room. By now most of the mice had fallen, and the few that were left were running away. Only the Mouse King remained, his sword still in his hand. I prayed that the Nutcracker would have the strength to fight with him.

"It is between the two of us," the Nutcracker called.

"I will never give up," the Mouse King said in a haughty squeak. "You must kill me to win." And with that he pounced foward on his flat, pointed feet and lunged at the Nutcracker.

"Back, Clara, back!" the Nutcracker cried.

Let him win, I said over and over in my mind. I could hardly bear to watch as the Nutcracker and the Mouse King chased each other around the room, their swords clashing. All the decorations on the tree were watching with me. I saw the Angel on the top of the tree lift her wings and fly to a lower branch so she could see what was going on.

"Who will win?" I asked her. I was sure angels knew ahead of time what was going to happen.

"The one who deserves to," she said.

How could that not be the Nutcracker? Even though I didn't know why he and the Mouse King had become such enemies, I knew he deserved to win. I noticed Sylvester watching the battle, too. "Whose side are you on?" I asked him.

"The Nutcracker's, of course," he replied. "Don't worry, Clara. He will win because you love him. . . . No one loves the Mouse King, not even his subjects. They're just afraid of him."

Above us the huge chandelier, which Mama had imported from Venice, trembled, its glass pieces clinking together. Mama would die if anything happened to her beautiful chandelier! For a moment I almost wondered if I should wake Mama and Papa, but then I remembered the Nutcracker saying that he must win this battle alone, without anyone's help.

The clock chimed, and again, as the owl peered out, Uncle's face flashed into view. "Uncle!" I cried. "Help us! Help the Nutcracker to win!" Uncle D. had created the Nutcracker. Surely he wouldn't let him be vanquished. But as soon as I spoke, my Uncle's face vanished and all that was left was the owl, his beak half hidden by a drooping wing.

I had thought that all the mice had vanished, but suddenly three of them appeared and wrested the Nutcracker's sword from his hand. He cowered backward as the Mouse King advanced upon him. "Stop!" I cried and, without thinking, took up a candle and hit the Mouse King on the head.

"Vicious girl!" he snarled, staggering back, his crown toppling. And just as he turned to seize me, the Nutcracker grabbed the sword that had fallen to the ground and ran the Mouse King through.

"Our king, our king!" the mice squeaked in frightened, angry voices. "He's killed our king!"

"Begone, or I'll do away with all of you," the Nutcracker said. He stooped down and took the Mouse King's crown from his head. "I've waited a long time for this moment," he said, and fell. As the mice carried their king away, I crept closer to where the Nutcracker lay, so still and stiff. Was he dead, too? My heart was beating with fear.

Suddenly Uncle appeared. I clung to him. "Is he dead?" I cried.

"For you I will bring him back to life," Uncle said and bent over the Nutcracker so that for a moment he disappeared from sight. When I saw him again, there he stood, no longer a Nutcracker but a handsome prince, all dressed in white.

"You have broken the spell," he said. "That was why I needed to kill this evil monster."

I looked around for the Mouse King, but he had vanished. "Where is he?" I asked.

"I let his countrymen take him away to bury him," the Nutcracker said. "He is a king, after all. He deserves a proper burial. He put up a good fight."

"He might have killed you," I said, remembering how close it had been and how the Nutcracker had lost his sword.

"But for you, Clara," he said. "I knew you wouldn't let me down."

How handsome he was! At least as handsome as the young man Sophie had danced with at the ball! And he was looking at me not as though I were a little girl, but as though I were a beautiful young woman. "Now you can't crack nuts anymore," I said. "Do you mind?"

He smiled. "Yes, I can." And taking a handful from his pocket, he cracked

them one after the other. "I am not any different than before. I just look different to the world. But you always saw me as I really was. You liked the way I looked even when I had a funny face and a big jaw."

I blushed. "Yes," I admitted, "because the expression in your eyes was kind."

"Your eyes, too, were beautiful. That was how I knew you were really a Princess, even though you seemed to be just a little girl."

"But I'm not!" I said. "I'm still just Clara."

The Nutcracker took my arm. "No," he said. "Now, for tonight, you are a Princess. Look at yourself!" He led me to the long mirror in the front hall. It was true.

"I look beautiful!" I said in surprise.

"This is how you will look later," he said.

"But what time is now?" I asked anxiously. "Is it later now?"

"For tonight it is." He took me in his arms, and we danced together, as close as two people who have always been one. I knew then that I loved him. "And now I want you to come with me to my own land, my kingdom. They all know about you and want to meet you."

"How *can* they know about me?" I said. "I've never been there."

"I told them," he said.

As we turned, I looked up at the Christmas tree. The angel had flown back and was perched at the top of the tree again. The decorations were once more tucked into the branches. Everything looked the same. There was no way Mama could tell anything out of the ordinary had happened, when she awakened in the morning.

"And the soldiers?" I said, looking around the room. "Where did they go?"

"They are all back in Fritz's room," the Nutcracker said. "They fought bravely and well."

"Fritz would be proud of them," I said. But I was glad he had not been awake to share this adventure with me, that it was mine alone. "Do I need my coat?" I said. "Will we be going outside?"

"You will stay warm," the Nutcracker said, "close to me." He waved his hand, and a golden sleigh appeared, a small one, just big enough for the two of us. He helped me into it, and we sat with our arms around one another. It was true. I didn't feel cold at all, even though, as we glided out the door, the snow was falling in big wet flakes that melted as they touched the ground.

How beautiful it was! All around us were huge fir trees, heavily covered with thick snow. Some of them were decorated, just like our Christmas tree, but the decorations seemed alive and moved as we came near, calling out to us. I saw a deer peeking out from behind a bush, but she just gazed at us with large gentle eyes. "Have you been here before?" I asked.

"Many times," said the Nutcracker. "This is my country. . . . This is where I used to live before the Mouse Queen put a spell on me."

"You said you would tell me that story," I said, sinking back against his shoulder. "Will you tell it now?"

"Certainly," he said, "if you're not too tired from the night's adventures to listen."

"I don't feel tired at all," I said. It was true. Even though I'd hardly slept, I felt as though I could travel all night.

"I HAD AN ORDINARY CHILDHOOD," the Nutcracker said, "just like yours, Clara. I had brothers and sisters, we played, fought, just like brothers and sisters everywhere. But what made my childhood so wonderful was that my Father was a toy maker. In fact, his name was Drosselmeyer, just like your Uncle."

"I wonder if they're related," I said. My Uncle had never mentioned a family like that.

"I believe they were," Nutcracker said. "If it weren't for your Uncle, I wouldn't have come to your house, and we would never have met."

"I think we would have met," I said. "I think we were destined to meet."

The Nutcracker squeezed my hand and looked at me lovingly. "Yes, you are right," he said. "It was destined, but I never knew that until tonight."

"You were going to tell me why you became such an enemy of the Mouse King," I reminded him.

"Yes," said the Nutcracker. "But it all started long ago, before I was even born. It was in the kingdom of Nuremberg, not far from here. A beautiful princess was born."

"What was her name?" I asked eagerly.

"Pirlipat. . . . She was her parents' only child, and they had been waiting for a child so long that when she was born, they were delighted."

"Was she beautiful, even as a baby?"

"Very. She had golden hair, large blue eyes, delicate features. The King and Queen adored her, just as your parents adore you, sweet Clara."

It's true. I know how happy my parents were to have a girl. Mama has told me that Papa said to her, the night I was born, "This is the best present I could have." But I wasn't beautiful like Pirlipat! I was a funny looking baby with a big round face and hardly any hair at all. I'm glad Nutcracker didn't see me then.

"There was only one thing the King and Queen were frightened of," Nutcracker went on, "and that was mice. Not just mice in general, but the Mouse Queen."

"The mother of the Mouse King?"

"Yes, but he hadn't even been born then."

"Then why was she angry at them?" I asked.

"Well, the King, like all kings, wanted his palace to be clean and beautiful. He became annoyed that mice were always scurrying about, stealing food. Sometimes they were so bold they ran right out in the middle of the kitchen and stole bacon and bowls of pudding. One day they even carried off a large cake the King had ordered to celebrate the royal anniversary!"

"They carried off a whole cake?" I asked. "How could they?"

"Oh, there were hundreds of them! Remember, the palace was huge, and the mice had been there for many, many years. They probably thought of it as *their* palace. They had thousands of little nooks and crannies to hide in, and each year they got bolder and bolder. But stealing the anniversary cake was the last straw. A hundred of them carted it off and devoured it down to the last crumb. When the King found that out, he went on a rampage. 'Get rid of all those mice!' he roared. 'I don't want a single mouse left in this kingdom.' And he hired my Uncle Drosselmeyer, a famous inventor, to create as many ingenious traps to catch the mice as he could. Ordinary traps would not work because these mice were so clever. Uncle Drosselmeyer built trap after trap, cunning ones, ones that no one could see, and one by one the mice vanished. Those that weren't caught, hid. The Mouse Queen was furious! One day she found the last of her seven sons dead in one of my Uncle's traps. In her rage she vowed to revenge his death. "You'll pay for this!" she told the King.

"Why didn't she get caught in a trap herself?" I asked.

"She was too clever. No matter what kind of trap Uncle devised, she saw through it. Oh, once, the tip of her tail got caught, but she nipped it off and ran away. You see, she thought the Palace was hers! She had dreams of a day when the King and Queen would go away and she and her family would reign supreme. She imagined them sleeping in soft white feather beds, dining on every kind of delicious cheese: cheddar, Camembert, Gruyère, Stilton . . ."

"But what could she do?" I asked. "Just one mouse against the King?"

"The day her last son died, she sent the King a message. 'Wait,' she wrote in her tiny mouse handwriting. 'I'll put a curse on your newborn child.'"

"How scary!" I was glad I hadn't been around to know her, though I could sympathize with how sad she must have been to have found all her children caught in traps.

"The King was terrified," Nutcracker said. "He knew how shrewd and implacable the Mouse Queen was. And the poor Queen of Nuremberg was hysterical. She cried every night. She even thought of sending her daughter to some far-off land where the Mouse Queen could never find her. But the King thought that was cowardly. 'We can't be frightened by a mere mouse,' he said. And he devised ways to protect the baby. Six nurses and six cats surrounded her every moment of the day and night. These cats were special hunters, known to be quick to pounce on a mouse whenever they saw one."

"That was clever," I said.

"Yes," Nutcracker agreed, "but, alas, not clever enough. One night all six nurses and all six cats dozed off. You see, from living in the castle, the cats had gotten sleek and overfed. They were no longer the ravenous, lively hunters they had been. They just lay about all day, licking their whiskers, lapping up bowls of heavy cream, munching on tender filets of fish."

"We have a cat," I said, "but she doesn't eat *that* well. Only sometimes I give her snacks."

"These cats looked like dogs, they'd gotten so overstuffed and lazy . . . And so one night the Mouse Queen, who'd been biding her time, snuck in and leaped on the cradle before anyone even saw her and brought a curse down on Pirlipat. When the nurses woke up in the morning and peeked into the cradle, they saw that the beautiful princess had turned into the ugliest baby on earth, with big bulging eyes and a huge mouth."

"Poor thing," I said. "She must have felt terrible."

"Not then. The Princess was just a baby, too young to look in mirrors. It was her parents who were upset. 'How will she find a husband?' they cried. 'Who will want her?'"

"But if she was a nice person," I said, "maybe someone would have wanted her even so."

"Perhaps," Nutcracker agreed, "but the King and Queen didn't think so. And, of course, they wanted their daughter to marry someone very special. In his rage the King called for Uncle Drosselmeyer, who had invented all those wonderful mouse traps. 'It's all your fault, you fool,' he said."

"But it wasn't really," I said.

"I know. But the King had to blame someone. 'If your traps had been really good, we would have caught the Mouse Queen herself.'

"'I tried,' said Uncle Drosselmeyer. 'I did my best. We did catch hundreds of mice.'

"'Not good enough!' yelled the King. 'What good did it do to catch hundreds when *she* went free?' And then he laid down the law. Of course, being a King, he could make up laws to suit himself. 'Reverse the spell and make the Princess as beautiful as she was before,' he said, 'or you will be killed.'"

"That wasn't fair," I said.

"Not at all," said the Nutcracker. "But what could Uncle Drosselmeyer do? He thought and thought and cogitated and cogitated."

"Is cogitating different from thinking?" I asked.

"It's more complicated. . . . You only cogitate when you've tried thinking and it doesn't work. He called in the court astronomer, and they spent days drawing up charts, looking in crystal balls, gazing at horoscope signs. They were willing to try anything! And one day they got this message: the spell could only be broken by a young man who had never shaved and had always worn boots and who could crack the rare Crackatook nut. The moment the Princess ate the kernel of that nut, she would be beautiful again."

"That doesn't sound so bad," I said. "I thought he'd have to slay a dragon or something."

"Well, if it had been a walnut or a Brazil nut or a pecan, then it would have been easy. But no one knew where to find a Crackatook nut! Have you ever seen one?"

"Never," I admitted. "I've never even heard of them."

"Each year for fifteen years," Nutcracker went on, holding my hand, "my Uncle set sail for another country. And in each he asked everyone he met if he had seen or heard of the Crackatook nut. But no one had. At times my Uncle was close to giving up, but he knew that the moment he did, his life would be forfeit. Because the King never forgot. In fact, as his daughter grew older, she, too, realized she was ugly, and it made her sad and angry. No one wanted to play with her. She had no boyfriends. Eventually the King and Queen had her educated at home. With no companions, she grew miserable and spoiled. Her actions accentuated her ugliness. If only she had tried to be a thoughtful and lovable person, she might have had as many friends as she wanted. But she didn't realize that. Every time she saw herself in a mirror, she hurled it across the room. She broke dozens of mirrors! But, of course, that didn't do any good."

I felt so sorry for the poor Princess. When I look in the mirror, I'm rarely totally pleased with what I see, but sometimes I am a little. Imagine never having a good day, a day when you looked nice. That would be sad!

"One day," Nutcracker continued, "Uncle Drosselmeyer stopped in on the way back from one of his journeys to visit his brother, my Father. We hadn't seen him for so many years, we didn't recognize him at first. We had just heard he was a very famous man who had moved to the castle and whom the King trusted above anyone. Because the King made sure no one outside the castle knew what had happened to his poor daughter."

"Were you glad to see him?" I asked.

"Very glad, dearest Clara. And he was glad to see us. The children had been babies when he last saw us. I was now eighteen, almost a man. My Uncle kept exclaiming over it. 'You must have many girlfriends,' he said."

"Did you?" I asked, trying not to be jealous.

"No, not a one," Nutcracker said. "I was shy, then. . . . Girls didn't seem to like me."

"Oh, I bet they did," I said. "But maybe they were shy, too."

"Perhaps. But my Father explained that we were a large, close family and that he was hoping I would become a toy maker, like him. He told my Uncle how good I was with my hands, how I helped him make toys when he was behind in his orders. 'And you should see him crack nuts!' my Father said. 'He's like a nutcracker.'"

"Is that how you got your name?" I asked.

"No . . . or at least it was just a nickname that my family used to tease me. Well, after dinner my Father took my Uncle into his toy shop. It was a clutter as always, full of half-finished toys, boxes, scraps of material, many kinds of wood. And on one shelf in a corner my Uncle spied a beautiful set of tiny boxes inlaid with pearls. 'How beautiful!' he said. 'Who has commissioned these?'

"'Oh, those are for myself,' my Father explained. 'I couldn't bear to sell them. I bought them many years ago from a nut-seller who had acquired them in Tibet. Inside is a nut he said was called the Crackatook nut.'"

"Your poor Uncle!" I cried. "If only he'd come to see your Father earlier. He would have saved himself all that trouble."

"True," Nutcracker said, "but at that moment my Uncle was beside himself with joy. Here he'd stopped off just for a friendly family visit and he'd found the very thing he'd been searching for for so many years. He hugged my Father, he hugged all of us children, he danced around with joy. Then he turned to me, 'Can you crack this nut?' he asked.

" 'Of course,' I said.

" 'Then we must set off at once,' said my Uncle and we did."

"But how did you know you could do it?" I asked.

Nutcracker laughed. "I didn't. . . . But how could I let my Uncle down? I knew I had to try. I would save my Uncle's life and, as a reward, marry the Princess."

I scowled. "Marry her!" I cried. "You didn't mention that part of the story."

Nutcracker looked embarrassed. "That was the reward," he said. "Whoever could restore the Princess to her original beauty, could have her hand in marriage. That was what the King had decreed."

"But what if you hadn't liked her?" I said, not enjoying this part of the story at all. "She might have been beautiful but mean! I would never agree to marry someone I had never met."

Nutcracker kissed my cheek. "You are wiser than I was, dear Clara. All I thought of was how exciting it would be to marry a beautiful Princess, to be hailed as a Prince."

"But it didn't work out?" I said, watching him intently.

"Alas, no. We went to the castle, my Uncle and I, and immediately set off to see the Princess."

"Was she ugly?" I said hopefully.

Nutcracker nodded. "As ugly as you can imagine. . . . Not just her looks, but you see, her parents had spoiled and indulged her so much, it had twisted her character. She looked at me with hateful eyes. 'How do you like him,' her Father asked. 'Will you marry him, my darling?'

" 'Oh yes,' the Princess cried, dancing up and down. 'He's gorgeous!' " At that Nutcracker blushed.

"Well, you are," I said. "It's not your fault, as long as you don't get vain."

"Never fear. . . . My Uncle brought forth the Crackatook nut, and I took it between my teeth. In one second—crack! crack!—I had shattered it into tiny bits! The Princess reached for the kernel greedily. 'Mmmm,' she said, closing her eyes. 'It tastes wonderful.' "

"And did it make her less ugly?" I asked anxiously.

"It was amazing," Nutcracker admitted. "In one second she was transformed into the most beautiful young girl you can imagine, with flowing golden hair, blue eyes, skin like silk. . . . Almost as beautiful as you, Clara."

This time I turned red with embarrassment. "And did she lose that mean expression in her eyes?"

He sighed. "No, that did not change. But I admit, I was so taken by her beauty, by the change in her appearance, I didn't notice. I stepped forward to kiss her and claim her as my bride. And suddenly, out of nowhere, the tiny Mouse Queen came darting forth. I didn't even see her until it was too late. I stepped right on top of her!"

"Good!" I cried. "It served her right."

"That is true," Nutcracker said, "but as she was dying, she hissed, 'Some day my newborn son will avenge my death, Nutcracker! Beware, beware!' And at the very moment of her death, I changed as miraculously as the Princess had. I was no longer a handsome young man of eighteen. My head grew large, my eyes bulged, my mouth reached from ear to ear. I had been changed into a Nutcracker, just as you saw me. The Princess let out a shriek. 'Marry *him?*' she cried. 'He's ugly. He's hideous.' She thought nothing of my feelings. 'Take him away.' she shrieked. 'I want to marry a real Prince!'"

"You're lucky you *didn't* marry her," I said. "She sounds awful." I leaned against him. "Anyway, she was wrong. You weren't ugly. Your eyes were always kind and intelligent. If I had been her, I would have married you anyway."

Nutcracker tightened his hold around my waist. "That was what the court astronomer said. . . . He took me aside and predicted that I would never regain my true self until I had killed the Mouse Queen's son and found a young girl who would love me, in spite of the way I looked."

I wondered if my Uncle had known that story when he gave me the Nutcracker for a present. I decided to ask him the next time I saw him. "You were the best present I ever got," I said, gazing at him with love and admiration.

"Now I am glad about the Mouse Queen's son," Nutcracker said, "because I know we belong together. I would never have been happy with the Princess, even if she had consented to marry me."

"You would have been miserable!" I said. "She was mean and cruel and selfish."

I HAD BEEN SO FASCINATED by the Nutcracker's story that I had hardly noticed where we were going. The golden sleigh in which we sat glided softly over the snow, sometimes rising into the air. No horses drew it along. It seemed to move effortlessly on its own. And although the snow continued to fall softly all around us, I felt as warm as though I were indoors.

"The air smells so wonderful!" I said. "Where are we?"

"This is my country," the Nutcracker said. "Soon we will be home, and you will meet my parents, my sisters and brothers, and all the people who live here."

I looked down and saw a river rushing below, bright orange and smelling of the sweetest fresh juice. The fruits that hung on the trees seemed frosted with sugar, so glistening and ripe they were like stars. Everywhere I looked, small creatures peeked out to watch us pass by. I saw many of the creatures from our Christmas tree, but alive and moving around. There were Stefan and Sylvia, with their flock of sheep. Stefan was sleeping under a tree, but Sylvia saw me and waved.

"Are we far from my home?" I asked Nutcracker. I worried suddenly that Mama might wake up and find me missing.

"Don't worry," he said. "Your parents are fast asleep, having wonderful dreams."

"Just like me," I said. "This seems like a dream, and yet it's real." I touched him to make sure he was real, and his arm was as warm and solid as my own.

Below, pink swans sailed to and fro, their sinuous necks bent gracefully to one side. "I didn't know swans could be pink," I exclaimed.

"They can be any color you like," Nutcracker said. "What is your favorite color?"

I hesitated. "Blue," I said. "Light blue."

Hardly had I said the words when the swans turned the loveliest shade of pale blue. Everything was blue, the trees, even the snowflakes falling to the ground. The Nutcracker looked pleased when he saw how delighted I was. "Why, look," I cried. "There's Sylvester. I didn't know you would allow mice in your kingdom."

"Sylvester is a friendly mouse," Nutcracker said. "He isn't related to the Mouse King or Queen. He escaped from them long ago and prefers to live here with us."

Gradually the sleigh began to slow down and sank gently into the ground. The moment it did, a group of people came running toward us, four beautiful girls and an older woman with snow-white hair and an affectionate expression. They were all dressed in delicate silver gowns, more beautiful even than the ones Mama and her friends had worn at the dance. I knew these must be some of the Nutcracker's subjects. They kissed and hugged both of us, as though they had been waiting for us for a long time.

"This is Clara," Nutcracker said, taking my hand and presenting me to all of them.

"We are so happy to meet you at last," one of them said. "We have heard all about how you have freed our Prince from the terrible spell."

"Well, I didn't really do that much," I said. That was true. Except for rushing up to get Fritz's soldiers and hitting the Mouse King with a candle, I'd spent most of the time hiding!

"Tell us," one of them begged, "how it all happened."

Nutcracker told the story. He made me sound so brave! "I had fallen to the ground, wounded," he said, "and then Clara went and got me something to drink. That gave me the strength to go on."

"What was the Mouse King like?" another asked.

"Gigantic and fierce," Nutcracker said, "and very nimble with his sword. For a moment I was afraid he would get the best of me. And then Clara hit him with a candle!"

"Bravo, Clara!" they cried and hugged me.

"He staggered backward," Nutcracker went on, "and fell to rise no more." He unbuckled the sword from around his waist. "Now I no longer need this."

"You must come into the palace," a young girl said. "We have planned a big celebration for both of you."

No one said I was just a little girl and that it was long past time for me to have been in bed. I walked beside the Nutcracker into the palace, my arm linked in his. I danced with some of his subjects while he stood watching me with pride. I felt like a real Princess. "Do you like it here?" he whispered. "Would you like to live here with me forever?"

"Oh, yes," I said. "I never want to leave."

I knew my parents would be sad not to see me, but perhaps they could come to visit. Even Fritz could come, if he promised to leave his soldiers behind. To my surprise I saw all my dolls, gathered in a group, even poor Claire, whom I haven't played with in so long. They seemed to forgive me for that and just waved gaily as I passed by.

"Now," said Nutcracker. "It is time for the ceremony to begin."

"What ceremony is that?" I asked. I was looking with awe at the long white pillars of the palace, the sparkling, many-colored glass windows.

"You must become my Princess," he said. "Will you?"

"Of course," I replied, a little nervous. "What do I do?"

"Wait here," he said, and a moment later he appeared with a beautiful gold crown covered with tiny jewels. He was already wearing one on his own head. "Will you be my Princess and live here with me forever?" Nutcracker asked.

"I will," I said, bowing my head.

He placed the crown on my head; everyone cheered. I thought of Pirlipat and how foolish she had been. If she had only loved the Nutcracker as he was, she would have been here now instead of me, and his eyes would have been fixed lovingly on her instead of me. What a silly girl! Probably now she's married to some dull old king whom she can't stand and they don't even know what to say to each other.

"How does it feel to be a Princess?" Nutcracker asked as we sat down on the large thrones that were placed side by side on a raised platform.

"I don't feel any different," I said with surprise. "I thought I would change somehow."

"I don't want you ever to change," he said, smiling at me tenderly. "Now, you must touch each couple, and they will come to life and dance for us."

In front of me were a pair of Spanish dancers, a man and a woman. The woman had a fan, just like the one Sophie had used, and her black hair was piled regally in an upsweep. I reached out and touched her shoulder, and when she looked up into my eyes for a second, I thought it was Sophie. Everything had been so strange tonight. Surely Sophie was at home asleep and I would see her tomorrow for Christmas dinner. Or would I? I touched the man dancer, too, and then sank back on my throne next to the Nutcracker.

"Will I be home for Christmas dinner?" I asked him.

"You will be where you want most to be," he said. "This dance is in your honor, Clara. Watch!"

Where I wanted most to be. I knew I wanted to be with the Nutcracker forever, and yet did that mean I would never see my parents or Sophie or Fritz or Uncle Drosselmeyer again? I thought of my Uncle, working so hard on his puppets. Wouldn't he be surprised to know that they were real, not just puppets but real people who could talk and move and dance?

The Spanish dancers whirled in front of us, leaping high in the air. Would they really not have come to life unless I touched them? "Do you like them?" the Nutcracker asked.

"Yes, they're wonderful."

The Spanish dancers knelt down before us. "We welcome you, Clara," they said in unison and disappeared.

"Will there be more dancing?" I asked.

"In a moment, but now, surely, you are hungry and thirsty. . . . Let us go inside, and you will meet my Father. He is down in his toy shop. He spends all his time there. He loves his work more than anything. Everything you see here he has created, but it can only come to life at the touch of a loving hand."

Nutcracker's Father had a kindly expression. His skin was wrinkled and he stooped a little as he came forward to greet me. "You are even more beautiful than I had imagined," he said. "I have always wished for my son to meet a girl like you."

"Thank you," I said.

"I was afraid he would never come back to us," he went on, "and I cursed myself for having allowed him to go off with my brother. I should have kept him safe at home."

Nutcracker embraced him. "But see, Papa," he said, "it all worked out. You will never have to worry again."

"Parents always worry," his Father said. "Clara knows that, don't you, my dear? Even when you are grown, we still think of you as children, needing our care and protection."

I wished so much that Mama and Papa could be there to see me at that moment! Would they recognize me in my crown and my splendid pink dress? I

imagined their surprise and delight. Fritz would grumble and fuss and say I looked just the way I always did. I looked around the toy shop. "I hope you don't make soldiers," I said. "My brother has so many of those already."

"I make whatever toys children like to play with," the old man said. "Dolls, music boxes, tops."

"You've made some wonderful dolls," I said. "I enjoyed playing with them, but now—"

"Now you are ready to move beyond that," he finished for me. "Don't apologize, my dear. That time comes for all of us. But, luckily for me, there are always more children coming along to enjoy what I create."

"Come to the great hall with us, Papa," the Nutcracker said. "The Chinese dancers will appear soon. You've always loved them."

"Yes," he agreed, walking beside us. "I have always wanted to make a trip to the Orient. Instead I content myself with creating these Chinese dolls."

"And fans," the Nutcracker reminded him.

"I got one of those for Christmas!" I said. "Did you make it?"

He nodded.

Then perhaps my Father had met the Nutcracker's Father! Perhaps they were friends! "I wish my parents were here," I whispered to the Nutcracker as we climbed back on our thrones. "They would be so pleased."

As an answer he just took my hand and held it. It felt warm and good. I left my hand in his as I turned to watch the Chinese dancers.

They were such funny little creatures in little pointed hats. She wore puffed-out pants and golden slippers. They moved back and forth, stiffly like kittens playing with a ball of yarn. "Princess! Princess!" they called out.

While we watched, a woman approached with a silver tray and offered us something to drink. Since the Nutcracker took a goblet, I took one too and raised it to my lips. The drink had a sweet, fizzy taste. Was it wine? But now that I was grown-up, I could drink wine, if I wanted. I sipped it slowly and munched on some of the small iced cakes that had come with it. Suddenly I realized I hadn't eaten since supper time and that so long ago! I thought of eating with Fritz, just soup and bread and milk before the party, trying to decide what dress to wear, going up to change.

When the Chinese dancers had finished, the Nutcracker called them over. "I want you to meet Clara," he said. "She has come from far away to be with us."

"We are honored," the Chinese man said.

"Have you liked our dancing?" asked the Chinese woman.

"Oh, yes," I said.

At that they bowed low and retreated.

A moment later four harlequins came dancing out. They looked so familiar! Where had I seen them before? At the Christmas Eve party! I remembered Uncle D.'s big dolls and how I had sat beside Sophie and watched them dance. And then, just as that thought came into my head, Uncle D. himself appeared. He was far off, in the crowd of people watching the dancers, but it was definitely him. I could tell because he was dressed just as he had been at the party, in a tall black hat with silver stars on it. What was he doing here? I wondered. I wanted to rush over and talk to him, but that would have been rude in the middle of the dancing, so I sat quietly, waiting for it to be over.

When the harlequin dancers had finished, I turned to the Nutcracker. "My Uncle is here!" I said.

"Where is he?" he asked. "I would like to meet him."

"Why, he's right over there," I said, but when I turned, he had vanished. "Maybe I was wrong. . . . But I was sure I saw him."

"Perhaps he went away for a bit," the Nutcracker said. "Not everyone likes dancing. He will return."

I wondered if Uncle D. would recognize the Nutcracker. He had made him, he said, and fixed him when his head came off and then turned him into the prince. "You must know my Uncle," I said. "He made you in his workshop."

"I don't really remember," Nutcracker said. "All that seems so long ago."

"Do you remember the Christmas tree?" I asked. "And the doll bed that I put for you to sleep in?"

He squeezed my hand. "Yes, and you wrapped me up in the blanket and talked to me so I wouldn't feel afraid."

"I thought you would hate our family after you were hurt at the party," I said.

"Never," he said. "Anyway, all that is over. Everyone has moments of suffering and fear, but in the future we will always be together."

I gazed at him, hoping that would be true. "Yes."

The next dancers were Stefan and Sylvia. Only now they were as large as I was. Stefan was playing his little pipe and he had the same impish gleam in his eye. I wondered who was watching their sheep, and then I saw that all the sheep had gathered and were quietly watching the dance with their big gentle eyes. Stefan disappeared for a moment and Sylvia danced alone. She was so pretty I almost felt jealous as I saw the Nutcracker look at her so intently.

"She's my friend," I told him.

"I know."

Then suddenly who should appear but the Mouse King! I was so frightened I grabbed the Nutcracker's arm. "I thought he was killed!" I cried.

"Don't worry, darling Clara," said the Nutcracker. "It's all pretend."

I wondered what he meant. Surely that was the Mouse King! He had the same fierce eyes and crown, the same mean expression. And then suddenly he took his head off, and it was Stefan after all! He had just taken a head that looked like the Mouse King in order to fool us. I laughed from relief.

"I was so frightened," I admitted.

"The Mouse King will never return to bother us again," the Nutcracker said. "He is far away, in his own country."

"Stefan, why did you do that?" I said. "You shouldn't play tricks like that."

"He's terrible," Sylvia said affectionately. "He loves to fool around." She slipped the mouse head under her arm. "Come off, you rascal," she said, pulling his arm.

Then there were more dancers, Russian ones this time. They whirled in the air so fast it made me dizzy. To tell the truth, I was beginning to get sleepy. I knew it wouldn't be polite to yawn, so I tried to cover my mouth with my hand. I remember how Mama said it was hard for queens and kings to go to so many ceremonies. People expected them to be always regal and grand, never irritable or tired. Even the crown seemed heavy on my head. Could I take it off when I went to sleep?

I saw Nutcracker looking at me with concern. "Are you getting tired, Clara, dear?" he asked.

"A little," I admitted. "But it's been beautiful, wonderful. Thank you for arranging it all."

One of the Nutcracker's subjects stood before us and offered me his hand. "Shall I?" I asked, and Nutcracker nodded.

I danced all around the room, changing partners. I wished so much it was Nutcracker I was dancing with! How I yearned for him! As I whirled around, I seemed to glimpse some of the people I had seen—the Spanish lady, the angel, the Chinese couple. Sometimes I lost sight of Nutcracker and became anxious. He seemed to fade away and then reappear.

As I stopped finally, out of breath, my Uncle appeared before me.

"Uncle!" I cried. "I thought I saw you before, but then you went away. Isn't it wonderful here? Isn't this a beautiful place?"

My Uncle bowed low before the Nutcracker. "But now it is time to return," he said.

"What do your mean?" I cried, startled. "Return where?"

"To your home, to your parents." He held out his hand.

I clung to the Nutcracker. "Is that true?" I said. "Do I have to go?"

"You must choose," he said. "If you want to stay, you can."

"Oh, I do," I said. "I don't want to leave you. I promised I would stay forever."

The Nutcracker got up. "We have not danced yet," he said. "Let us dance now."

He took me in his arms, and we danced all around the large room. He danced so well, and I felt so secure and happy and safe in his arms. If I left, we would never dance together again. "I'm afraid my Uncle will make me go back with him," I murmured.

"You can always return," Nutcracker whispered.

"Can I? Will you still be here?"

"Of course," he said. "We will be here forever."

"And you won't marry anyone else, if I go away?" I asked.

"How can you ask that?" he said. "We are betrothed."

As we danced, I wondered what I should do. I wanted so much to stay! In this country there was no school, no one to give me orders, to tease me, to tell me what to do. I could sleep as late as I wanted. But most of all, my beloved Nutcracker would be beside me all the time. We could talk, tell each other stories. Really, I knew so little about him, and he knew very little about me. It seemed as though we had just begun to know each other.

As the music stopped, I turned and saw my Uncle watching us. I had almost hoped he would have disappeared again.

"I want to stay," I told him. "I can't bear to go back."

"But your parents," Uncle said. "Think how grieved they will be! How will I explain it to them?"

"Why can't they come here?" I asked.

"That is impossible."

I thought of my parents crying, wondering where I had gone, never seeing me again. Without thinking, I threw myself into my Uncle's arms. "Oh, let me stay," I begged. "I want to so much!"

"But you are forgetting the most important thing of all," Uncle said.

I looked at him in surprise. "What is that?"

"You must finish your childhood, dear Clara."

As he spoke, I looked down, and instead of the lovely pink dress, I was wearing my white nightgown again. The crown was gone from my head. "But I'm not a child!" I cried.

"Soon you will be a young woman," he said, "but not yet. It takes time."

Time, time . . . The words seemed to echo in the huge room, like the chiming of a clock. I turned to Nutcracker. He was dressed just as he had been before. "Can you forgive me?"

"I have parents, too," he said. "I understand . . . And, it is true, Clara. To me you seem like a young lady because you are so wise and so beautiful. But part of you is still a child."

"We can take the golden sleigh," my Uncle said. "You will lend it to us, won't you?" he asked the Nutcracker.

Nutcracker looked sad as we left the palace. He put his arm around me, and I leaned against him. "We will see each other soon again," he said.

"Will we?" How did he know that?

My Uncle seated himself in the sleigh and beckoned to me to sit beside him. I turned to the Nutcracker one final time, and he embraced me, kissing me softly on the lips. Then I let myself slide out of his arms. I began to cry.

"I don't want to go home," I said, hiding my face against my Uncle's shoulder. But then I realized the Nutcracker was still standing, watching us, so I dried my tears with the sleeve of my nightgown. The sleigh began to lift itself into the air, and gradually the Nutcracker became smaller and smaller. "Goodbye," I called down. "I love you."

"Goodbye," the Nutcracker called, his voice getting fainter and fainter. "Goodbye, Clara . . ."

I DON'T REMEMBER THE TRIP home with my uncle as well I remember the trip with the Nutcracker. Maybe we went faster coming back, or maybe I was so sleepy by then that I didn't look. Perhaps we went home by another way. All I know is that I must have really fallen asleep because when I opened my eyes, there was Mama, shaking me.

"Clara," she said, "what are you doing down here on the floor?"

I looked around the living room. There was no sign of the fight of the night before. The big tree stood beside me, just as always. I saw the Nutcracker, asleep in the doll bed. "I came down to keep the Nutcracker company," I said. It was strange; he had turned back into an ordinary toy, but in some ways I was glad. No one but I would know who he really was. Mama might be angry if she knew all that had happened.

"But you're not a child anymore," Mama said, still sounding annoyed. "Sleeping on the floor! You probably didn't sleep a wink all night! And it's Christmas Day!"

I jumped up and hugged her. "I slept wonderfully," I said. "I never slept better in my life. Do I look tired?"

She looked at me carefully. "No, not really. . . . Well, when you're young, you can sleep anywhere, I suppose."

"Is Uncle D. here?" I asked. I thought perhaps he had slept in one of the extra rooms since we had gotten back so late.

"It's just nine in the morning," Mama said. "Why would he be here?"

I shrugged. But I could hardly wait to see my Uncle again. He would remember better than I how we had come home. Where had he put the golden sleigh? I wondered. Perhaps it went back magically by itself.

"It's almost breakfast time," Mama said. "Hurry and put on your robe. There's hot chocolate and muffins. Fritz has been up for hours. He said he came down and saw you, but you were so sound asleep, he decided to leave you there."

Had Fritz noticed that his soldiers were put back differently in the box? But when I went in to breakfast, he just waved at me. "Have a good night on the floor?" he said.

How jealous he would be if he knew all the excitement he had missed! "Yes, I slept very well," I said.

"I had the craziest dream," Fritz said, reaching for a muffin. "I dreamed my soldiers were in a real fight."

"Who were they fighting?" I said, trying to look innocent.

"I'm not sure. It was all mixed up . . . But they won! I'd trained them so well, you see."

Papa was pouring coffee for himself. "Well, Clara," he said, "I hope your nutcracker appreciates your staying up with him all night."

"He does," I said. Thinking I needed to add something further, I said, "It was his first night in our house. I was afraid he might be lonely."

"You know, I was like that," Papa said. "Some of my toys almost used to seem real to me. I would talk to them and imagine them talking back."

"*I* never do that," Fritz said. "I know they're just toys."

We had a nice breakfast, and afterward I went up to my room, carrying the nutcracker in his bed. I knew it wasn't the real nutcracker, just a toy, but I was glad, still, that he would be with me even as a doll till the time we would be reunited at last.

Later in the day we all went to visit my Aunt Helen and Uncle Charles and Cousin Sophie. It had snowed the night before, and outside there was so much snow, you could hardly walk. Fritz made snowballs and threw them at the trees until Papa made him stop. The carriage pulled up right in front of our house, and we all snuggled in under the blankets.

I liked the ride. The sky had cleared and was bright blue. We saw many families out visiting. I had the nutcracker tucked in the pocket of my coat. I wanted to show him Sophie's house.

As soon as we got there, Sophie came running out. I was wearing the dress she had given me. "How pretty you look!" she said. "You look better than I ever did in it!"

But she looked lovely, her hair swept up, her cheeks bright pink with excitement. "I could hardly sleep last night," she confided. "I'm always like that on Christmas Eve. The night seems so long!"

I told her how I had slept downstairs under the tree. I thought of telling Sophie all my adventures of the night before, but I decided not to. The only person I would tell would be Uncle. He had been there so he would remember it all.

"Where is Uncle D.?" I asked. "Has he come yet?"

"Why no," Sophie said. "I don't think so . . . Mama, when is Uncle coming?"

"In time for dinner," my Aunt Helen said. "I think he said he was bringing an extra guest."

"Who?" I cried excitedly.

"His nephew from Nuremberg . . . It's his first trip to the city. He's just eighteen."

My heart started beating faster. I looked at the tall grandfather clock, wanting the time to pass quickly. The long table was already set, and delicious smells were coming from the kitchen.

Then, as we were sitting under the tree, looking at the presents, the bell rang. A moment later in walked Uncle D. with his nephew. I ran over to my Uncle and hugged him. "I'm so happy to see you!" I cried.

"But we parted just a moment ago," my Uncle said. "Or so it seems." He smiled. "Clara, I want you to meet my nephew, Nathaniel. He has come to the city, and I've been telling him all about you."

I turned red. Then I looked at Nathaniel. He was tall and slim, and he smiled at me in such a friendly way, as though he knew me. He looked a little like the Nutcracker. "You are just the way I imagined you," he said.

I had thought he would want to stay with Sophie since she was closer to his age, but he sat next to me at supper. "I've wanted to come here for so long," he said, "but we are a big family and don't have much money."

"What does your father do?" I asked, sipping my juice. Uncle always gives us cranberry juice because it looks like wine.

"He makes toys. . . . He says that his is a profession that is always needed. People never stop having children and children never stop wanting toys."

Usually boys don't like to talk to me that much, but Nathaniel was as talkative and relaxed as though he had known me forever. I liked the way he looked. He had green eyes, and, though he wasn't handsome exactly, he had the sort of face that made you trust him. I found myself telling him all about my life, about school and my friends, about my family.

"Some day you must come and visit us," he said. "We hear so much about you from Uncle. My sisters would love to meet you, too."

"I would love to come," I said. I glanced over at my Uncle, who was at the other end of the table. If only I could get him alone!

After dinner there was to be dancing, just as there had been at my parents' house. I felt a little sad, knowing I would have to just watch, as always. I went up to Sophie's room to help her get ready. She changed into her dancing slippers.

"How nice Uncle's nephew seems!" she said. "You seemed to get along so well together."

"Yes, it was strange," I said. "Usually I feel shy with boys."

"But when you meet someone special, it's different," she said. "Then you never run out of things to say."

"Was it like that with the man you danced with last night at our party?"

Sophie nodded. "I wish he could come today . . . But I'll see him again, I know."

When she was ready, we went downstairs together. A young man came rushing up and asked Sophie to dance almost the minute we appeared in the doorway. Then I saw my Uncle standing alone in the corner.

"Did you get home all right last night?" I asked him. "I was worried about you."

"Of course I did." He looked at me. "And how is the handsome nutcracker I gave you?"

"Oh, he's fine. He told me all about how he and the Mouse King came to be enemies. Now I know everything!"

"I was going to tell you that story today," Uncle said, "but if you know it already . . ."

At that moment Nathaniel came up and bowed in front of me, "Would you like to dance, Clara?"

I looked at my Uncle, as though asking for his permission. He had said I had to finish my childhood, after all. I wasn't sure if he would think it was all right. "Go off," he said. "Don't lose any time when they're playing such a beautiful waltz."

I stepped into Nathaniel's arms. He was a good dancer, almost as good as the Nutcracker had been, light and graceful. "I can't believe I am here finally," he said, looking around the room. "I've imagined it for so long. It's like a dream."

"Yes," I said. "It is like a dream."

CAST LIST

Act I

Drosselmeyer	Alexander Minz
Mr. Stahlbaum	Gayle Young
Mrs. Stahlbaum	Sallie Wilson
Clara	Gelsey Kirkland
Fritz, Clara's brother	Warren Conover
Grandmother	Ann Barlow

Guests .... Amy Blaisdell   Janet Shibata
Sara Maule   Patricia Wesche
Ruth Mayer   Sandall Whitaker
Berthica Prieto

Victor Barbee   Richard Schafer
William Carter   Raymond Serrano
Michael Owen   Frank Smith
Marcos Paredes

Children .... Brian Adams   Kirk Peterson
Carmen Barth   Jaime Roque
Peter Fonseca   Christine Spizzo
Aurea Hammerli   Denise Warner
Susan Jones   Cheryl Yaeger

Servants	Maia Rosal Gary Cordial
Harlequin	Gregory Osborne
Doll	Rebecca Wright
Moor	George de la Pena
Nutcracker/Prince	Mikhail Baryshnikov
King of Mice	Marcos Paredes

Mice .... William Carter   Michael Owen
David Cuevas   Richard Schafer
Vladimir Davidov   Raymond Serrano
Rodney Gustafson   Frank Smith
Charles Maple

Toy Soldiers .... Brian Adams   Robert LaFosse
Warren Conover   Gregory Osborne
George de la Pena   Kirk Peterson
Peter Fonseca   Jaime Roque
Roman Jasinski   Scott Schlexer

Snowflakes .... Cynthia Harvey   Jolinda Menendez

and Elizabeth Ashton   Lisa Lockwood
Carmen Barth   Sara Maule
Michele Benash   Hilda Morales
Amy Blaisdell   Berthica Prieto
Nancy Collier   Cathy Rhodes
Fanchon Cordell   Lisa Rinehart
Laurie Feinstein   Maia Rosal
Cynthia Gast   Janet Shibata
Aurea Hammerli   Kristine Soleri
Alina Hernandez   Christine Spizzo
Janne Jackson   Carla Stallings
Susan Jones   Denise Warner
Lucette Katerndahl   Patricia Wesche
Francia Kovak   Sandall Whitaker
Elaine Kudo   Rebecca Wright
Elizabeth Laing   Cheryl Yaeger

Act II

Court Buffoons . . . . Rodney Gustafson	Eric Nesbitt
Charles Maple	Gregory Osborne

Spanish Dance . . . . Jolinda Menendez	Clark Tippet
Chinese Dance . . . . Hilda Morales	Kirk Peterson
Shepherds . . . . Aurea Hammerli	Warren Conover
Russian Dance . . . . George de la Pena	Roman Jasinski
Waltz . . . . Nanette Glushak	Marie Johansson
Victor Barbee	Richard Schafer

and Patrick Bissell	Robert LaFosse
Gary Cordial	Michael Owen
David Cuevas	Jaime Roque
Vladimir Davidov	Scott Schlexer
Peter Fonseca	Raymond Serrano

Carmen Barth	Cathy Rhodes
Cynthia Gast	Janet Shibata
Cynthia Harvey	Christine Spizzo
Francia Kovak	Denise Warner
Sara Maule	Patricia Wesche

CREDITS

Costumes	Frank Thompson
Director of Photography	Larry Boelens
Associate Producer	Lois Bianchi
National Philharmonic	
Conducted by	Kenneth Schermerhorn
Chorus	Boys of Desborough School
Chorus Master	Roger Durston
Music Producer	Andrew Raeburn
Choreography for The	
Snowflake Waltz	Vasily Vainonen
Narrator	Norman Rose
Videotape Editors	Gary Princz
	Max Curtis
Production Assistant	Bettina Brooks
Assistants to the Producer	David Krawitz
	Remi Saunder
	John P. J. Toland
Assistant to Mr. Baryshnikov	Jurgen Schneider
Assistant to Mr. Charmoli	Richard Beard
Assistants to Mr. Aronson	Lisa Jalowetz
	Irving Milton Duke
Costumes executed by	Barbara Matera
Scenery executed by	Theatre Techniques, Inc.
Puppets by	E. J. Taylor
Wardrobe	May Ishimoto
	Robert Boehm
Pianist	Steven Rosenthal
Ms. Kirkland's hair	
designed by	Patrik D. Moreton
Assistant to Mr. Thompson	David Murin
Production Manager	Barrie Diehl

Our thanks to National Ballet School of Canada

Recommended by The National Education Association

Facilities by Glen-Warren Productions

The end

Every fly saw a smile on her beautiful face

As the wind carried her off without leaving
  a trace.

Ten thousand compound eyes shed tears
  of joy that day,

When the fly who couldn't fly rose up and
  flew away.

Her paper-thin body began to tremble,

And a great thrill spread among the flies all assembled.

As they watched in amazement, the wind lifted her high,

And held her aloft in the bright summer sky.

So old was she now, so thin and so frail,

A wonderful thing happened as her voice began to fail.

A wild wind whipped through the neighboring trees,

Singing through branches and blowing the leaves,

Just remember, my loved ones," she said to them all.

"We each have a purpose, if we but hear the call.

Life is short but it's sweet, and full of wonder, too,

And I'm truly not sad that I never once flew."

Two weeks passed, then three and then four,

She outlived her brothers and sisters and more.

Now old and wise, younger flies loved her so.

Then one summer day she said, "Dear friends, I must go.

And she did learn to dance, as well as to sing,

And found a wonderful life, without any wings.

And as the days of her life rapidly faded,

She became the happiest fly ever created.

So the little fly walked on with her head held high,
And loved what she saw of the earth and the sky.
And because she was walking, she found tasty tidbits
Of all sorts of things that the flying flies missed.

Love your life, my dear daughter, and you'll never
    go wrong.

Love each precious moment of life's sweet song.

Be a loving fly while you still have a chance,

If you can't soar in the sky, you can sure as heck dance!"

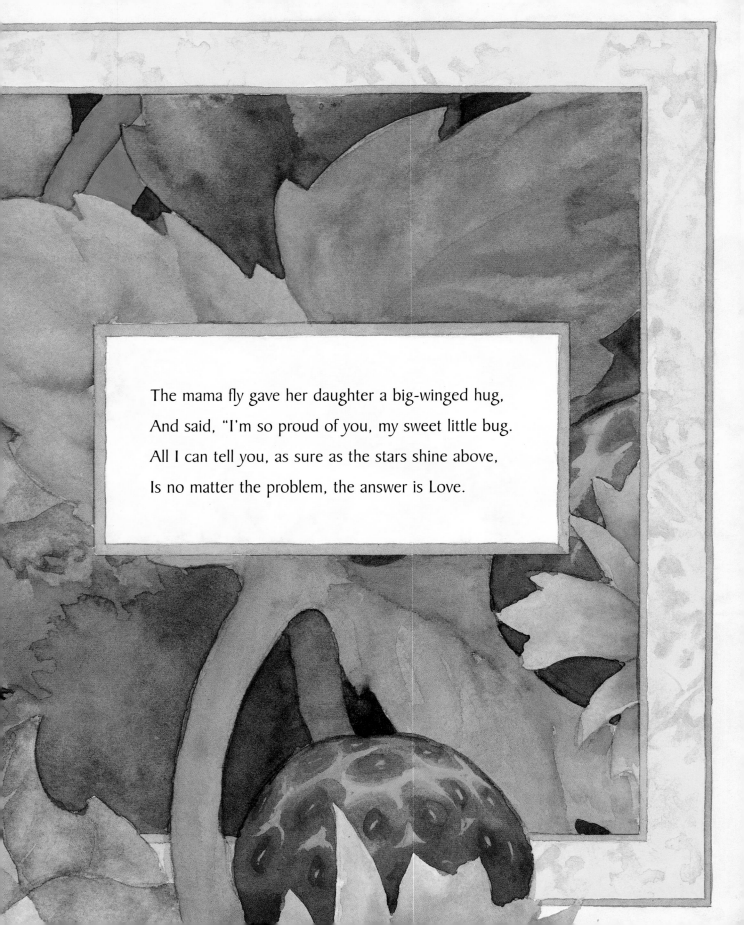

The mama fly gave her daughter a big-winged hug,
And said, "I'm so proud of you, my sweet little bug.
All I can tell you, as sure as the stars shine above,
Is no matter the problem, the answer is Love.

Nor wishing I could trade with anyone else,

Nor feeling ashamed of being myself.

But before I walk on in my uncommon way,

Is there any more wisdom you can give me today?"

The little fly listened very thoughtfully,

And said, "Thank you, dear mama, you've deeply moved me.

I shall spend no more time in bitter tears,

Nor useless regrets, nor runaway fears,

The younger fly whispered, "Please, tell me more,
What did the Great Mother of Life make me for?
If I'm a fly who can't fly, then what will I do?"
Her mama replied, "I can't solve that for you."

"That is your mission, your own special quest,
To find for yourself the things you do best.
Don't waste time regretting things you can't do.
We flies live three weeks, sometimes just two!"

"The Great Mother of Life does not make mistakes,
Even when it seems like we've gotten bad breaks.
Life is much more than flying, I promise you, dear.
Give up your sadness, and give up your fear."

And she sobbed and she sobbed, like no fly ever had.
"Dear daughter," said her mother, "I know you feel bad.
But wings are not everything, they're just two little parts.
You've got a good mind, and you've got a good heart."

Hidden from view, she cried with a sigh,

"A fly who can't fly, what good am I?

Am I really a walk, or a jump, or a sit, or a see?

Because certainly 'fly' is the wrong name for me."

Her mama, still watching, heard every word,

And flew to her side just as quick as a bird.

Startled and teary, the younger fly moaned,

"Oh, mama, I'm of no more use than this stone!"

Her sisters and brothers buzzed all around,

While she jumped and she jumped, always dropping
back down.

She finally gave up, and walked sadly away,

To a spot in the shade near a rock that was gray.

But when it came time for their wings to unfold,

(This happens when flies are but seven days old),

Mama Fly noticed a strange and sad thing:

One of her daughters didn't grow wings!

Her compound eyes both shone red and bright,

And her six legs looked fine, as she stood upright.

But when one by one all the other flies flew,

She looked confused and helpless, not knowing what to do.

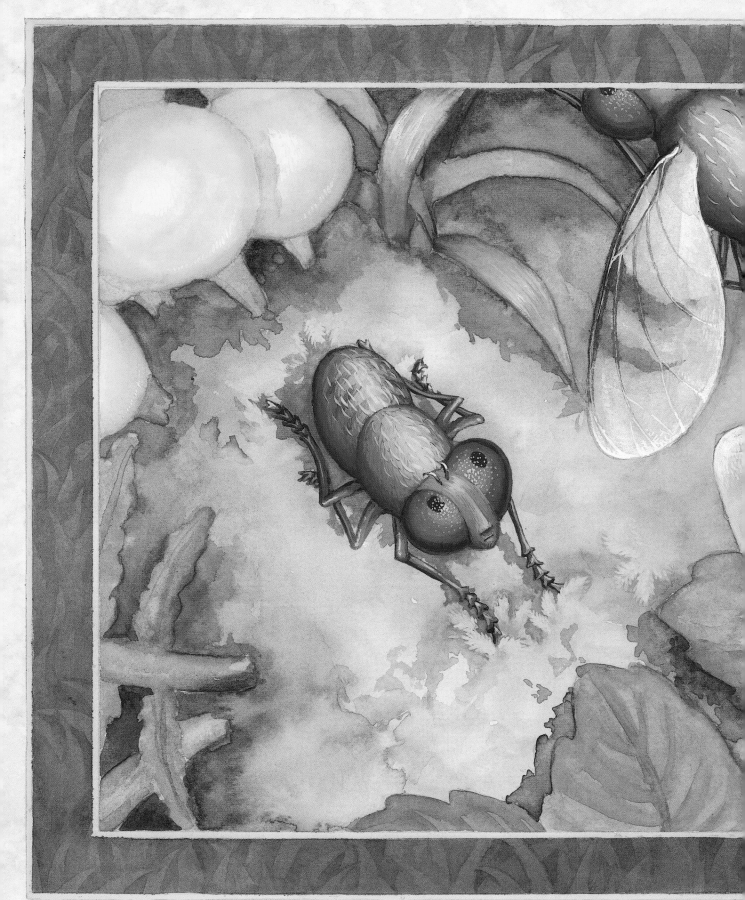

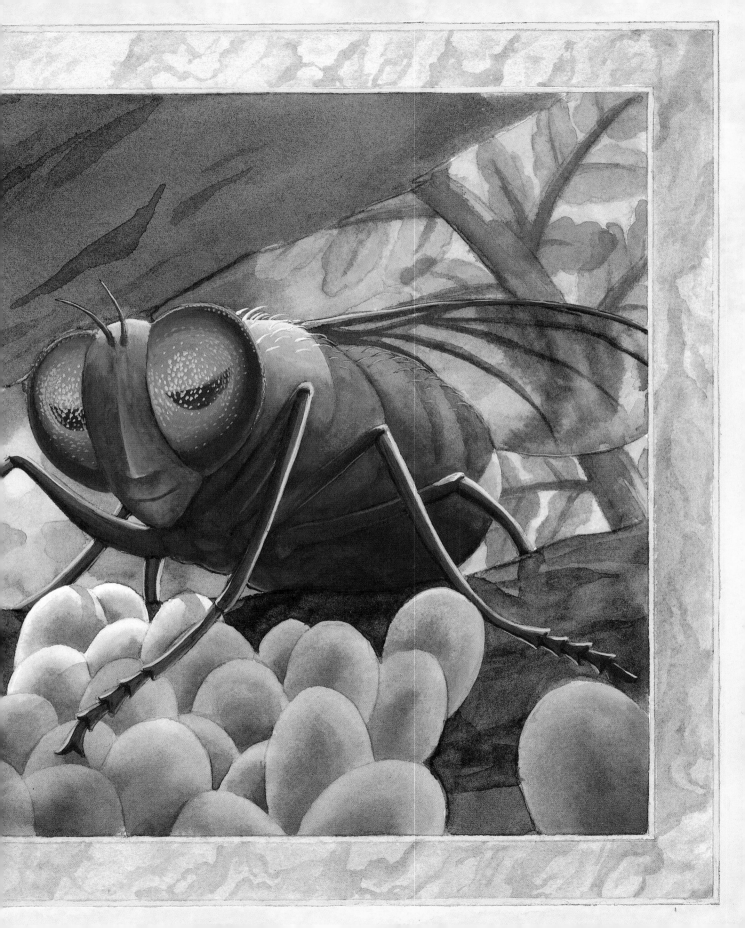

She was born as an egg to a double-winged mother,
Along with fifty fly sisters and sixty fly brothers.
After hatching, they wriggled as cute as could be,
No difference between them that any could see.

Once upon a time there was a fly who couldn't fly.

Cover design by Grace Pedalino

Hampton Roads Publishing Company, Inc.
1125 Stoney Ridge Road
Charlottesville, VA 22902

434-296-2772
fax: 434-296-5096
e-mail: hrpc@hrpub.com
www.hrpub.com

If you are unable to order this book from your local
bookseller, you may order directly from the publisher.
Call 1-800-766-8009, toll-free.

Library of Congress Catalog Card Number: 2002101355

ISBN 1-57174-286-7

10 9 8 7 6 5 4 3 2 1

Printed in China

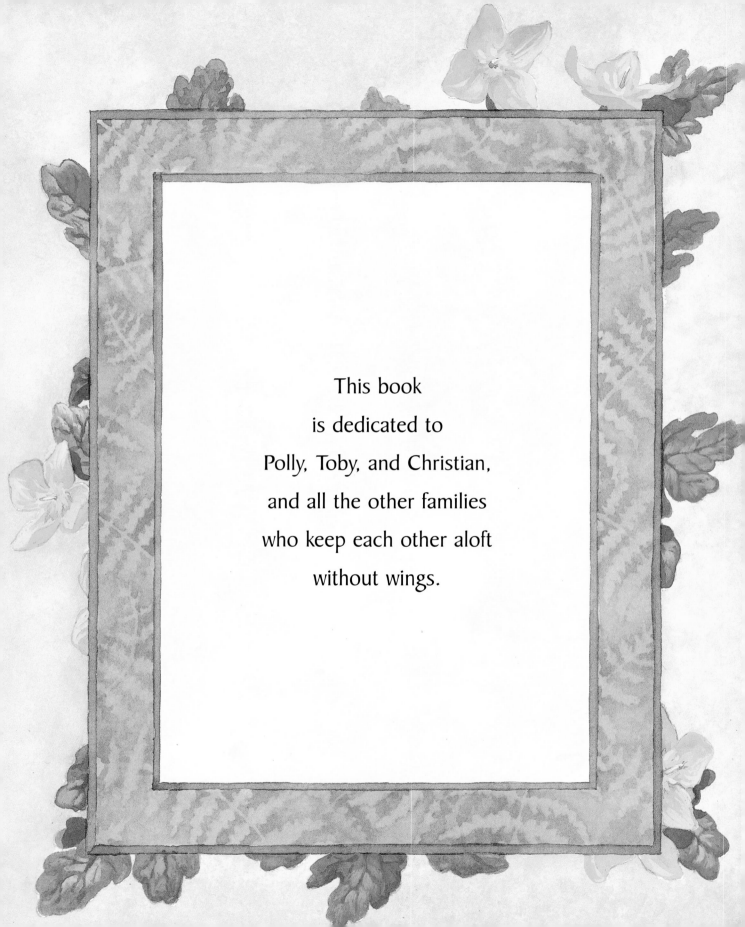

This book
is dedicated to
Polly, Toby, and Christian,
and all the other families
who keep each other aloft
without wings.

The Wonderful Life

of a

Fly Who Couldn't Fly

Bo Lozoff

art by Beth Stover

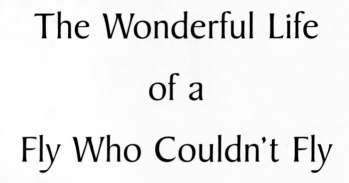

HAMPTON ROADS
PUBLISHING COMPANY, INC.